Ten For Me

by Barbara Mariconda

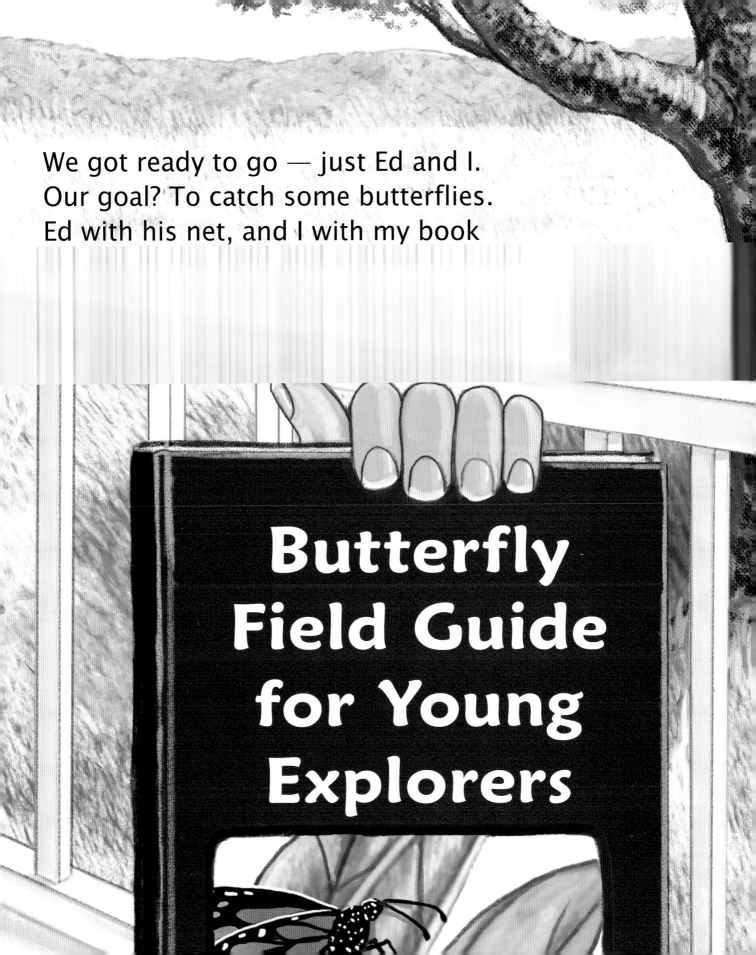

We got ready to go — just Ed and I.
Our goal? To catch some butterflies.
Ed with his net, and I with my book

Butterfly Field Guide for Young Explorers

That first day out, it wasn't much fun
'cause Ed netted ten and I netted none!
How many in all? Let's add them again!
"Well, 10 + 0 is 10," Ed said. "10 + 0 is 10!"

To attract butterflies, you need to provide a
food source (nectar or pollen) and a host plant
for the female to lay her eggs.

Fiery Skippers lay their eggs on tall grass.

Butterflies Captured and Released

Ed   Me

HHL HHL

That second day out still wasn't much fun
'cause Ed netted nine and I netted one!
"How many in all? Let's add them again!"
"Well, 9 + 1 = 10," Ed said. "9 + 1 = 10!"

Each butterfly species uses different flowers, grasses, or trees as their host plant. Caterpillars will eat from that special plant.

Butterflies Captured and Released

Ed

Me

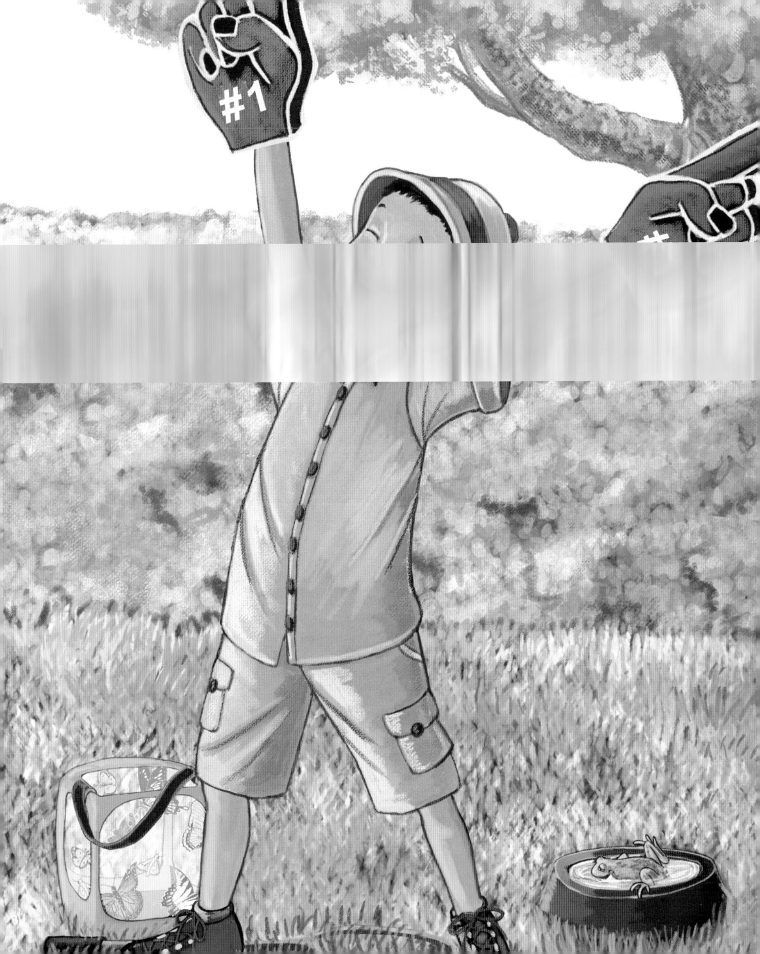

Butterflies Captured and Released

Ed	Me
ΙΙΙΙ ΙΙΙΙ ΙΙΙΙ ΙΙΙΙ ΙΙΙΙ ΙΙΙ ΙΙ	ΙΙ

Plants and butterflies have adapted together over thousands of years. Monarch butterflies use milkweed poison to protect themselves. Monarchs lay their eggs on milkweed.

That third day out, I was still feeling blue
'cause Ed netted eight and I netted two!
"How many in all? Let's add them again!"
"Well, 8 + 2 = 10," Ed said. "8 + 2 = 10!"

That fourth day out, I still couldn't see how Ed netted seven and I netted three! "How many in all? Let's add them again!" "Well, 7 + 3 = 10," Ed said. "7 + 3 = 10!"

Butterflies Captured and Released

Ed | Me
ᴬ

ᴴᴴ ᴴᴴ ᴴᴴ ᴴᴴ ᴴᴴ | ᴴᴴ ᴵ
ᴴᴴ ᴵᴵᴵᴵ

Some butterflies have ragged brown wings that camouflage them against dead leaves.

That fifth day out, I was still feeling sore
'cause Ed netted six and I netted four!
"How many in all? Let's add them again!"
"Well, 6 + 4 = 10," Ed said. "6 + 4 = 10!"

Question Marks and Red-spotted Purples
like the juice of over-ripe fruits.

Butterflies Captured and Relea

Ed	Me
ᜁ	ᜁ

Black Swallowtails lay their eggs on plants like carrots, parsley, dill, fennel, and Queen Ann's Lace.

Butterflies Captured and Released

Ed

Me

That sixth day out, I thought I would die!
'cause Ed netted five . . . and so did I!
"How many in all? Let's add them again!"
"Well, 5 + 5 = 10," we said. "5 + 5 = 10!"

That seventh day out, I used my new tricks,
and Ed netted four and I netted six!
"How many in all? Let's add them again!"
"Well, 4 + 6 = 10," I said. "4 + 6 = 10!"

Many butterflies nectar (drink nectar) from flowering plants.

Butterflies Captured and Released

Ed

Me

Some male butterflies puddle (drink from mud puddles) to get the nutrients they need.

Butterflies Captured and Released

❀ Ed	Me 🦋
HHI IHII HHI HHI HHI HHI HHI THH HHI HHI HHI THH II	THH HHI HHI IHII IHII THH III

That eighth day out, it felt just like heaven,
'cause Ed netted three and I netted seven!
"How many in all? Let's add them again!"
"Well, 3 + 7 = 10," I said. "3 + 7 = 10!"

That ninth day out, I really felt great
cause Ed netted two and I netted eight!
"How many in all? Let's add them again!"
"Well, 2 + 8 = 10," I said. "2 + 8 = 10!"

Question Marks and Red-spotted Purples
are attracted to barnyard smells!

Butterflies Captured and Released

Ed	Me

That tenth day out, it was my turn to shine
'cause Ed netted one and I netted nine!
"How many in all? Let's add them again!"
"Well, 1 + 9 = 10," I said. "1 + 9 = 10!"

If planting a butterfly garden, use plants that are native to your area.

Butterflies Captured and Released

Ed ☑️ | Me 🦋

That last day out, well, I did it again!
Poor Ed netted none, and I netted ten!
"How many in all? Let's add them again!"
"Well, 0 + 10 = 10," I said. "0 + 10 = 10!"

Butterflies Captured and Released

Ed

Me

55

55

And then we stopped and looked at our scores
to see which one of us finally caught more!
"How many for Ed? How many for me?"
"It looks like a tie!" Ed shouted with glee.
"But wait! What's this . . . ?

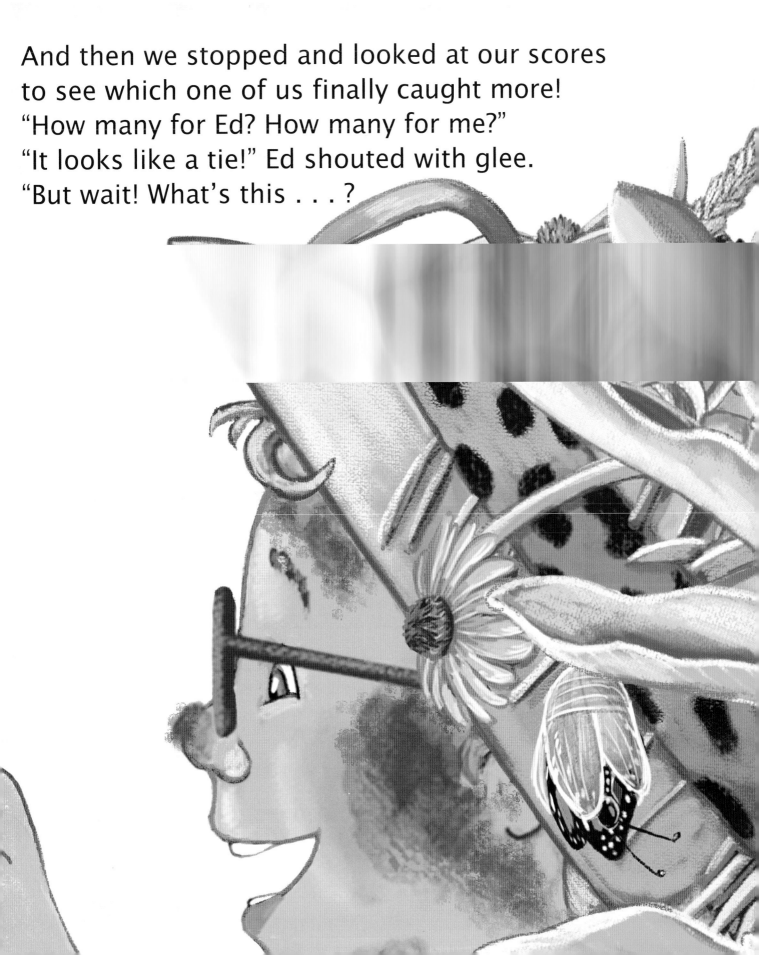

"Hey look, and see!
It looks like now the winner is . . .

...ME!"

For Creative Minds

The For Creative Minds educational section may be photocopied or printed from our website by the owner of this book for educational, non-commercial uses. Cross-curricular teaching activities, interactive quizzes, and more are available online. Go to www.SylvanDellPublishing.com and click on the book's cover to explore all the links.

Numbers and Patterns

What are some number combinations that add up to ten?

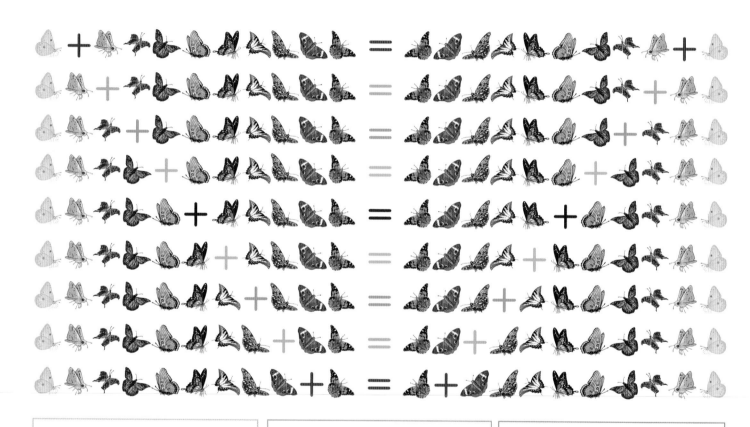

1 + ? = 10	2 + ? = 10	3 + ? = 10
4 + ? = 10	5 + ? = 10	6 + ? = 10
7 + ? = 10	8 + ? = 10	9 + ? = 10

Do you see a pattern in the number of butterflies that Ed and Rose caught and released each day?

Day	Ed	Rose	Total
one	10	0	10
two	9	1	10
three	8	2	10
four	7	3	10
five	6	4	10
last day	0	10 + hatchling	11
Total	**55**	**56**	**111**

Use the repeating pattern of butterflies shown below to identify the missing butterfly in each of the following patterns.

Butterfly Body Parts

Butterflies are insects. They do not have a backbone as we do. They have a hard, outer covering called an exoskeleton.

All adult insects have three main body parts: head, thorax, and abdomen.

The eyes, antennae, and mouthparts are on the head.

Wings and legs attach to the thorax.

The heart and body organs are in the abdomen.

Butterflies use their two antennae to "smell."

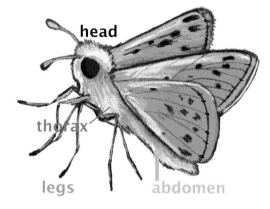

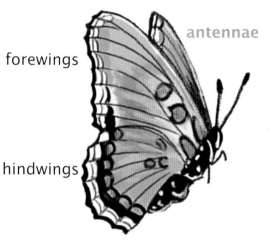

Their "mouths" (proboscis) are like curled-up straws that uncurl when they drink.

All butterflies have four wings: forewings in front and hindwings in back.

They have six legs and feet. Not all are easily seen. They "taste" with their feet.

Butterfly Life Cycle Sequencing Activity

Butterflies undergo a complete metamorphosis: a series of changes in the body form during their life cycle. Can you put the butterfly life cycle in order? Answers are upside down below.

Adult butterflies emerge from the pupa. They fly as soon as their wings unfold and dry. 	When fully grown, caterpillars turn into a pupa. A butterfly's pupa is called a chrysalis; a moth's pupa is called a cocoon. 
 Adult females lay eggs on host plants.	 Caterpillars (larvae) hatch from eggs. As caterpillars grow, they shed (molt) their hard outer layer and have a new, bigger one underneath. Most caterpillars molt at least four times.

Answer: May start with eggs or adults. General order is egg, larva (caterpillar for butterflies or moths), pupa, and adult.

Butterfly Compare and Contrast

How are the butterflies alike and how are they different? To compare the butterflies at different stages of their life cylces, by size, etc. see the free online activites.

Giant Swallowtail

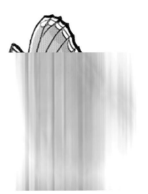

Red-spotted Purple

Common Buckeye

Clouded Sulphur

Question Mark

Fiery Skipper

Western Tiger Swallowtail

Painted Lady

Gulf Fritalary

For my friend Virginia Weir—as I tally up the blessings in my life, there you are again and again—BM

To my wonderful Mom who has always loved butterflies—SR

Thanks to Mary Santilli, Presidential Award Recipient for Elementary Mathematics (CT 1991) for verifying the accuracy of the math information in this book.

And thanks to all the butterfly experts who provided guidance and their expertise:
Karen Oberhauser, Project Manager of Monarchs in the Classroom
Kelly C. Lotts, USGS National Biological Information Infrastructure, Big Sky Institute
and to the many members of North American Butterfly Association (NABA) chapters:
 Bill Boothe, Hairstreak Chapter (FL Panhandle)
 Bill Haley, Tennessee Aquarium; President, Tennessee Valley Chapter
 Janice Malkoff, Cindy Jenkins and Sandy Koi of Broward County (FL) Chapter
 Eleanor Ryan, Eugene Springfield (OR) Chapter
 Linda M. Evans and Elane Neuhring, Miami Blue (FL) Chapter
 Yvonne Homeyer, Vice President, St. Louis Chapter

Publisher's Cataloging-In-Publication Data
Mariconda, Barbara.
  Ten for me / by Barbara Mariconda ; illustrated by Sherry Rogers.

    p. : col. ill. ; cm.

  Summary: Join two young children on a mathematical butterfly hunt. The number of butterflies caught each day always adds up to ten. Who will win? Learn how to attract a variety of butterflies through the plants and food they rely on and about their life cycles. Includes "For Creative Minds" educational section.
  Interest age group: 003-008.
  Interest grade group: P-3.
  Issued also as pdf reproductions in English and Spanish, as well as ebook with selectable English or Spanish text.
  ISBN: 978-1-60718-074-6 (hardcover)
  ISBN: 978-1-60718-085-2 (pbk.)
  ISBN: 978-1-60718-099-9 (English eBook)
  ISBN: 978-1-60718-110-1 (Spanish eBook)

  1. Addition--Juvenile literature. 2. Butterfly attracting--Juvenile literature. 3. Butterflies--Life cycles--Juvenile literature. 4. Addition. 5. Butterflies. 5. I. Rogers, Sherry. II. Title.

QA115.M33 2011
513.211   2010941279

Lexile Level: 460 Lexile Code: AD

Curriculum keywords: add/subtract, compare/contrast, equations/math symbols, life cycle: metamorphosis, number patterns, ordinal numbers, repeated lines, tens make friends

Manufactured in China, June, 2011
This product conforms to CPSIA 2008
First Printing
Published by Sylvan Dell Publishing
Mt. Pleasant, SC 29464

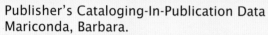